Lee Aucoin, *Creative Director*
Jamey Acosta, *Senior Editor*
Heidi Fiedler, *Editor*
Produced and designed by
Denise Ryan & Associates
Illustration © Claire Chrystall
Rachelle Cracchiolo, *Publisher*

Teacher Created Materials
5301 Oceanus Drive
Huntington Beach, CA 92649-1030
http://www.tcmpub.com
Paperback: ISBN: 978-1-4333-5448-9
Library Binding: ISBN: 978-1-4807-1127-3
© 2014 Teacher Created Materials

When I Grow Up

Written by Ella Clarke
Illustrated by Claire Chrystall

When I grow up, this is what I will do.

I will fly to the moon.

4

I will ride a wave.

I will sail a ship.

I will build a castle.